A **Topps** LEAGUE Story

THE 823RD HIT

· BOOK FOUR ·

By **Kurtis Scaletta**

Illustrated by **Eric Wight**

Amulet Books
New York

For Byron, our little champ
—K.S.

To Ethan and Abbie
—E.W.

Library of Congress Cataloging-in-Publication Data

Scaletta, Kurtis.
The 823rd hit / by Kurtis Scaletta ; illustrated by Eric Wight.
p. cm. — (A Topps league story ; bk. 4)
Summary: To keep Teddy "the Bear" Larrabee happy and slugging, Chad the batboy has to figure out what a crabby fan would be willing to trade for Teddy's lucky home run ball.
ISBN 978-1-4197-0446-8 (hardcover : alk. paper)
ISBN 978-1-4197-0445-1 (pbk. : alk. paper)
[1. Baseball—Fiction. 2. Batboys—Fiction. 3. Baseball cards—Fiction.] I. Wight, Eric, 1974– ill. II. Title. III. Title: Eight hundred and twenty-third hit.
PZ7.S27912Aap 2012
[Fic]—dc23
2012008321

Book design by Chad W. Beckerman

Printed and bound in U.S.A.
10 9 8 7 6 5 4 3 2 1

ABRAMS
THE ART OF BOOKS SINCE 1949
115 West 18th Street
New York, NY 10011
www.abramsbooks.com

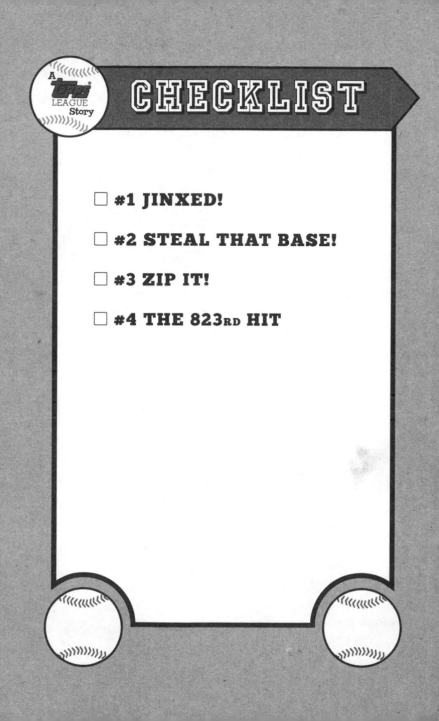

CHECKLIST

For two weeks in August I did the worst thing ever. I did something I never thought I'd do: I rooted against my team, the Pine City Porcupines.

This is what happened.

When I got my job as a Pines' batboy, Mom and Dad said I couldn't work during the school year. They said I'd be out too late on school nights. They thought I would need the time to do homework.

So I knew my days as a batboy were numbered when Mom started talking about

clothes and school supplies and my new teacher.

"Why can't I work on weekends?" I asked at dinner.

"We already agreed you wouldn't work during the school year," said Dad.

That was true. But I only agreed so they would let me take the batboy job.

"It's just a few games," I said. I took the Porcupines' schedule out of my pocket and spread it on the table. I stabbed the month of September with my finger. "The regular season ends in two weeks. The Porcupines are on the road for one of those weeks. Then they're in town for only one more weekend. After that, it's just the playoffs."

"How many games are we talking about?" Mom asked.

Now I knew I had a chance.

"Two," I said. "Three if you count Labor

Day, and four if you count Friday. Plus the playoffs."

"Hmm. That sounds like a lot of games to me," said Dad. "You could fall behind on your schoolwork and never catch up."

"Melissa Carvel was out of school for three weeks last year when she had the mumps," I said. "She caught up."

"That girl didn't have a choice," he said. "We do."

Dad won that round.

I went on to the next.

"If you don't want me to work on school nights, why do you make me walk the dog and unload the dishwasher?" I asked.

"Those things don't take you out of the house for hours," said Dad.

He was right. I knew it was a weak argument.

I decided it was time to play my best card.

"Dylan's parents are letting *him* work on the weekends."

Dad sighed. "You can work on the weekends until the Porcupines are done," he finally agreed. "But only under two conditions."

I felt a mixture of hope and dread. "What two conditions?"

"First, once school starts, you have to do all of your homework before you go to the ballpark."

"Of course." I wasn't worried. We didn't get that much homework at the beginning of the year.

"Second, if you try to argue your way into working on a school night, the whole deal is off."

Dad was smart. I had been hoping to wheedle my way into working one school night. He saw this coming a mile off.

"OK," I said. "It's a deal. I accept the two conditions. I won't even *ask* to work on a school night."

"No matter what," Dad said. "I'm serious, Chad."

"No matter what," I said.

• • •

The Porcupines were going to be in the Prairie League playoffs, for sure. Each of the top four teams earned a spot in the playoffs. Even if the Porcupines lost the rest of their games, they'd be in at least fourth place.

The Porcupines had never been in the playoffs since I could remember. Now that they were headed there, I would get to see the playoffs—and watch them from the dugout! I loved my job.

A few days later, I took a closer look at the playoff schedule. What I read made me groan.

In playoff tournaments, there's a thing called "seeding." The seeding determines who plays who, when, and where. When there are four teams, the best-ranked team plays the last-ranked team, and the second-best ranked team plays the second-to-last ranked team.

The Porcupines were probably going to finish in either first or second place. The top two teams would have home-field advantage for the first round of the playoffs, which would be a five-game series. That was great news for the Porcupines—but bad news for me.

The playoffs would be starting on a Wednesday night. That meant the Porcupines would play their home games on school nights, and then be out of town for the weekend! So the only way I could work a game during the playoffs would be if the Porcupines lost a bunch of games now and sank into third or fourth place. Then they would start the series on the road and play at home over the weekend.

That would also give me a chance to see the Porcupines win the first series! They could win one of the first two away games, then come home to win the next two. I could be there for the celebration. That would be awesome beyond belief.

I clenched my teeth. There was only one way for things to work out my way, and it meant betraying my favorite team.

I felt sick to my stomach doing it. I was the biggest Pines' fan in Pine City. As a batboy, I was part of the team. That made it twice as wrong to root against the Porcupines. But I couldn't help it.

I cheered to myself when the Pines went on the road and lost five out of six games, including three in a row to the Swedenberg Swatters.

I started to worry when the Porcupines came home and won three straight games against the Centralville Cougars. In the dugout I was all smiles and high fives and "Way to go!" and "First place, here we come!" I was glad the Pines were playing well. But I had my heart set on being there for some of the playoff games.

Now it looked like the Porcupines were headed for second place. I was miserable. I would miss the playoff games. Even worse, I had betrayed my favorite team for nothing.

Then the Rosedale Rogues came to Pine City.

It was my turn to help the opposing team. I walked into the visitors' locker room, and one of the Rogues asked me to relace his shoes. I was hunched over in the corner, and the players forgot I was there.

"Glad this is the last series in this crummy stadium," one of the Rogues said.

"It's the sorriest sight in the Prairie League," another player agreed.

"I don't like the showers here," said a third player. "The water's not hot enough, and there's no pressure."

What would they complain about next? That our grass wasn't green enough? That our baseballs weren't round enough?

I finished lacing the shoes and plopped them on the bench. The Rogues still didn't notice me. Not even the guy who owned the shoes.

"The food is pretty boring here too," he said.

"I miss the catfish fingers and hush puppies back in Rosedale," said another player. It was Damien Ricken. He had just been called up from Rookie League. Ricken was supposed to be a big-deal pitcher.

By the time the game started, I didn't care about seeding and school nights. I just wanted the Rosedale Rogues to lose. I wanted them to be sorry they ever came to Pine City. I rooted for the Pines with all my might. Unfortunately, the Rogues were on fire. They scored four runs in the first inning, before the Porcupines even came up to bat. Worse, Damien Ricken struck out the first three Porcupines batters and was back in the dugout before I knew it.

"So that's the competition?" he asked the Rogues' catcher.

"Yep," the catcher answered with a grin.

Damien noticed me watching.

"Hey, kid. Where are the good places to eat around here?"

"Um . . . I like the food here at the ballpark," I said. I wanted to make that clear.

"I don't eat while I'm pitching. What about restaurants?"

"The Pine City Café," I said. I liked the pizza place better, but grown-ups always liked the Café.

"Don't get your hopes up," the catcher said. "It'll be closed by the time we get out of here."

"Figures," said Damien. "This town is all pines and no city."

The guys on the bench cracked up.

I was fuming, but I kept my cool. "The pizza place is open late," I told him.

• • •

The Porcupines never caught up. They lost to the Rogues, 7–2.

The next night wasn't much better. It was my turn to work in the Porcupines' dugout. They were losing, 6–1, by the fifth inning.

"I'll be glad when we're done playing these Rogues," said Mike Stammer, the Porcupines' shortstop. He had just struck out for the second time that night. "I won't miss them a bit."

"Me, neither," said Tommy Harris. "The only thing I like about tonight's pitcher is that he's not Damien Ricken. Man, that Ricken guy has a good slider. I really hope we don't have to face him again this season."

"You'd better hope we *do* see them again," said Teddy Larrabee. Teddy was the first baseman. People call him Teddy "the Bear" Larrabee, because he's big and kind of hairy. "You'd better hope we see Damien Ricken's slider, too," he added. "We'll have to get past them to win the Prairie League championship."

"I was hoping we could sneak by when they weren't looking," said Wayne Zane.

"That's not what I meant," said Teddy.

"Just sayin'," said Wayne. Wayne was the catcher, and he *thought* he was the team comedian. He grabbed his bat and went to the on-deck circle while Sammy Solaris, the designated hitter, went to the plate.

Sammy got a base hit. The crowd cheered, but the Porcupines were still behind by five

runs. Wayne strode to the plate. Meanwhile, Teddy headed for the on-deck circle. I had his bat ready.

Wayne drew a walk. The crowd cheered louder. The Porcupines had a rally going!

The Bear swung on the first pitch. The ball went high and deep, straight down the right field line. It hit the foul pole, bounced off it, and went into the stands. Now, if a ball hits the foul pole, it's fair, even if the ball ends up in foul territory. That made Teddy's hit a home run! The crowd clapped and stomped. The Pines were still down by two runs, but they were coming back!

Sammy, Wayne, and Teddy circled the bases. We all met them at the dugout steps and traded high fives. Danny O'Brien went up to bat. Brian Daniels was on deck. I used to have trouble telling them apart. Now I could finally keep them straight.

"Chad, can you go get that ball back?" Teddy asked. "It's kind of a big one for me."

"What's big about it?" Wayne Zane asked.

I was wondering too. Teddy had hit home runs before, although not enough for this one to be a big number.

"That was my eight hundred and twenty-third hit," Teddy explained.

"No, it wasn't," Wayne said. "Not unless you hit about seven hundred in Rookie League. And if you had done that, you'd be in the major leagues by now—*and* be a shoo-in for rookie of the year."

"I'm not just counting professional baseball hits," Teddy explained. "I'm counting *every* hit."

"What, like high school baseball?" Sammy asked.

"High school, junior high, Little League— all of it," the Bear replied. "Every hit."

"Even T-ball?" Wayne asked.

"Even T-ball," said Teddy. "A hit is a hit."

"I have a follow-up question," said Mike. "What's the big deal about hit number eight hundred and twenty-three?"

"Well," said Teddy. "Today is August twenty-third. So . . . today is eight twenty-three. Get it?"

"Yeah. That is kind of a coincidence," Tommy said. He pronounced it "co-inky-dink."

"Also," said Teddy, "today is my birthday."

"Hey! Happy birthday!" Tommy shook his hand. "Wow—you do need to get that ball back."

"See?" Teddy looked at me. "Find out who caught that ball. Tell 'em I'll trade a new ball for it."

"Sure," I said. "I'll try."

3

I walked around in the grandstand beyond first base. Somebody out here had Teddy's lucky birthday baseball. But who?

There was a man sitting in the third row who looked like he'd been punched in the eye. I slid in next to him.

"Hi, I'm Chad the batboy," I told him. "Did you see what happened to the home run ball that bounced off the foul pole?"

"I reached for it and was sure I'd get it." The man shook his head sadly. "But I wasn't paying attention. Somebody stuck their elbow in my

face." He touched his eye and winced. "Is it turning black?"

"More like purple and green," I replied.

"I didn't see who got the ball," the man said. "Ask him." He pointed at a big, tall guy a few rows back. "He must have got it. He's closer to the sky than everyone else."

"Thanks. Sorry about your eye." I ran up the steps to the big, tall guy a few rows back.

"Hi, I'm Chad the batboy. Did you see who got the home run ball that bounced off the foul pole?"

"I was sure I had it," the big, tall guy said. His voice was low and booming. "It was almost in my hand. Then this little guy jumped up and snagged it away from me."

"That's too bad," I said. "Did you see who got it?"

"That's him over there." The big, tall guy

pointed one section over. "The one in the wool hat."

"Huh?" I only saw one person in a wool hat. He was a little old guy about the size of two peanuts stacked end on end.

"That's him, all right," the big, tall guy said. "He's little, but he's tough."

"OK. Thanks."

I headed toward the man in the wool cap. I was wrong about him. He was the size of *four*

stacked peanuts. Still, I couldn't believe he had outjumped the big guy. He must have really wanted that baseball!

"Hi, I'm Chad the batboy." I offered him my hand. He just looked at it, so I took it back. "I heard you might have gotten the home run ball that bounced off the foul pole?"

"It's my ball," the old man said. "I caught it fair and square."

"I know. I just wanted to ask—"

"Don't waste your breath!" he said. "Don't think I'm giving it to you because you're a kid. Go ahead and make big eyes and sniffle and cry. I'm keeping the ball."

"I'm not going to cry," I said. "I work for the Pines. Teddy Larrabee, the player who hit the ball, wants it back."

"Then he shouldn't have hit it so hard," the old guy said.

"We're not asking you to just *give* it back," I told him. "Teddy will trade you a new ball. He'll even sign it for you."

"It's not for trade."

"Please?" I said. "It would mean a lot to the Bear."

"It means a lot to me," the old man said. "I've been wanting to catch a home run ball for sixty years. I'm not waiting another sixty years."

"Come on." I explained how it was Teddy's birthday ball and how he had been counting his hits since T-ball. I told the man about the coinkydink of number 823.

"Nice story," the old guy said. "But I'm still keeping the ball."

"OK. Well, I guess I'll just tell Teddy he can't have his birthday baseball."

"That's exactly what you should tell him."

"Thanks anyway."

I went back to the dugout. I'd been gone almost a whole inning. The Porcupines were just coming off the field to bat again.

"The guy who's got it wants to keep it," I told Teddy. "He doesn't want to trade."

"Tell him I'll give him fifty dollars," said Teddy.

"Wow," said Sammy. "I'll give you one of my homers for fifty bucks. Heck, I'll go up and hit a new one in my next at-bat."

"I need that baseball," said Teddy. "Go tell him about the fifty dollars. And if he still says no, tell him I'll give him a hundred dollars."

"Teddy, for a hundred dollars I'll sew you a baseball," said Wayne Zane.

"Can I hear one twenty?" Sammy started in like an auctioneer.

"One twenty!" said Danny.

"One twenty, one twenty, one twenty,"

Sammy rattled off. "Do I hear one twenty-five?"

"One fifteen!" said Brian.

"You're going the wrong way," Wayne told him.

"But that's all I have," said Brian.

"Stop it!" said Teddy. "I'm the one buying back a ball. You guys stay out of it." He turned to me and said, "Tell you what—I'll write him a note."

Teddy disappeared for a moment and returned with a notebook. He flipped to the first blank page.

"What's the guy's name?"

"He didn't tell me," I replied.

"Dear sir," said Teddy. He poked his tongue out of his mouth as he wrote. He ended it with a big, fancy signature. Then he folded the note and handed it to me.

"Go give him this."

"All right. But I have to wait until the end of the inning." I was a batboy first, messenger second.

"Hey, Teddy. What's the notebook for?" Sammy asked.

"Nothing." The Bear shut the notebook.

"I usually don't have school supplies in my locker," Sammy added. "That's all."

• • •

I went back to the right field seats in the top of the seventh inning. When I got there, the man in the wool cap was gone.

I pointed to where the old guy had been sitting. "Is he coming back?" I asked a woman who was sitting nearby.

"I don't think so," she told me. "I think

he was worried about that baseball. He was muttering about kids trying to con it off him."

• • •

The Porcupines lost the game, 9–4, and the Rogues clinched first place in the league. They celebrated on the field. It was depressing.

"Some birthday," Teddy grumbled as he got dressed. "We lost the game, and I lost my lucky birthday ball."

"Maybe it's not that lucky. The first thing it did was get lost," Wayne pointed out. "Just sayin'."

"Yeah, maybe it's a bad-luck ball," said Tommy.

Teddy grabbed his notebook and wrote something in it.

"What're you writing?" Wayne tried to read over his shoulder.

"N.O.Y.B.," Teddy replied. He pulled his notebook away.

"Oooh," said Tommy. "The Bear says it's none of your beeswax, Wayne. Step back."

"Worst birthday ever," Teddy mumbled. He stuffed the notebook in his bag and left the locker room.

"We should've sung the birthday song or something," said Tommy.

"Ah, we'll catch up with him and take him out for pizza," said Wayne.

Dylan came back from the other locker

room, shaking his head.

"The Rogues think they're all that," he said.

"I know."

It was the least fun I had ever had at a ball game. To make things worse, it was my last game before school started.

Welcome back, Chad!" Ms. Henry said as I walked into my new classroom. She knew me from the school play two years ago, *Hansel and Gretel*. Ms. Henry had been the director. My friend Abby played Gretel. I played a tree.

"You should meet Casey," Ms. Henry said. "He's a big baseball fan, just like you." She led me over to a new kid. His hair hung down in his face. He wore thick glasses. He was also wearing a Rosedale Rogues jersey that was two sizes too big for him. But I figured

I would give the kid a chance. He was a fellow baseball fan, even if he did root for the Rogues.

"Chad, this is Casey. His family just moved here from Rosedale. Casey, Chad is a batboy for the Pine City Porcupines. Doesn't that sound like fun?" Ms. Henry smiled like she'd just matched up the two best friends of all time, and went off to talk to some other kids.

"The Porcupines?" the new kid said with a snicker. He pushed the hair out of his eyes. "The Rogues just swept them."

"Only two games," I said. "The Pines are still the best team in the Prairie League."

"No way," Casey said, shaking his head. "The Rosedale Rogues have the best record. First place, remember? Plus they've won the last two championships, and they're about to win a third."

"Only if they beat the Porcupines," I reminded him. Casey didn't back down.

"Don't make me laugh."

"You'd better laugh now, because in a couple of weeks all you'll be able to do is cry."

We went back and forth like that until class started.

• • •

Dylan was in a different class this year, so I was glad to see him at lunch. He had his nose stuck in a book.

"What are you reading?" I asked.

He showed me the cover. "I'm reading about cells," he said. "It's really interesting."

Who reads a science textbook during lunch? Answer: Dylan.

"You would really get along with my dad," I told him. "My dad also loves to read."

The new kid slid in next to me.

"The Rosedale Rogues probably have the best pitching staff in all of Single-A baseball," Casey said. He didn't even bother with a "Hi" or a "Can I sit here?"

"I guess you haven't heard of Lance Pantaño," I told him. "He pitched a perfect game this season."

"Pantaño got lucky." Casey waved his hand like he was brushing away a fly. "Damien Ricken has a lower ERA, a lower WHIP, and a better DIPS."

I didn't know what those were, but there was no way I was going to admit it.

"I've seen Lance throw over a hundred miles an hour," I told him.

"Ricken doesn't just throw hard. He carves up batters."

Casey spent the rest of lunch describing Damien Ricken's pitching. He demonstrated his famous slider using Tater Tots. "And that's just Ricken," Casey said. "I haven't even told you about the rest of the rotation."

He went off to clear his tray. I noticed that his jersey had Ricken's name and number.

"Who is that kid?" Dylan asked.

"Casey."

"He's like the you of the Rosedale Rogues."

"I'm not like that, am I?"

"You aren't as annoying," Dylan agreed.

• • •

Casey caught up with me again on the way home from school.

"Let's go through the lineup," he said. "Who bats first for the Porcupines?"

"Tommy Harris," I said.

"What's his OBP?"

"I don't know," I said.

"Well, with lead-off hitters, especially, you

have to look at on-base percentage, not just batting average," Casey said. "Jasper Davis is .366, which is pretty good. He's the lead-off hitter for the Rogues. Now, his OPS could be better . . . I think it's .617." He laughed.

I didn't get it. I'd have to ask my uncle Rick about OPS.

"Who bats second for the Porcupines?" Casey asked next.

"Myung Young," I replied.

"Oh, yeah," Casey said. "He's a great defensive player."

I couldn't believe he admitted that the Porcupines had something going for them.

"What's his OPS?"

"I don't know," I said. "I don't know about anyone's OPS, all right?"

Casey shrugged. "Fine. Do you want to come over and see my baseball cards?"

"You should come over to my house and see *my* baseball cards," I told him. I had thousands, some dating way back to when my granddad was a kid.

"I bet I have more cards," he said.

"Don't be so sure. I have a lot."

"I have forty thousand cards. How many do you have?"

"Forty thousand and six," I lied.

"Ha."

"Anyway," I said, "I have to go do my homework. If I don't keep up, Mom and Dad won't let me work the Pines' games this weekend."

"We didn't get any homework," Casey reminded me.

"I'm going to work ahead." The truth was that this new kid was driving me crazy. I never thought anyone could talk too much about baseball, but he did. Worse, everything was a contest. He was a bigger fan of a better team. He had more baseball cards. He used abbreviations I had never heard of.

"Come on, I don't have any friends in Pine City except for you," Casey said. "We just moved here last week. Dad's company transferred him out of the blue."

I sighed. "OK. I guess I can come over for half an hour."

"Let's go, then," Casey said.

On the way, he explained that his parents hadn't bought a house yet. They were all staying with his great-uncle Marvin. "He's a big baseball fan," said Casey.

"He sounds like my uncle Rick," I said.

"My granddad's even a bigger fan," said Casey. "He's the reason I have so many baseball cards. He's been collecting since he was a kid, and they're all in perfect condition."

Dylan was right. Casey *was* the me of the Rosedale Rogues. Casey even had a baseball-crazy uncle and baseball cards from his grandpa.

We arrived at a house with a big porch. An enormous black cat glared at us through the window.

"That's my uncle's cat, Arthur," Casey said with a shudder. "He's mean. Let's go around back."

We did. As soon as we walked in, we heard a baseball game on the radio. An old man was hunched over a crossword puzzle.

"Five-letter word for 'buffalo,'" he said. "That's easy: 'bison.'" His voice was familiar.

"Uncle Marvin, this is my new friend, Chad."

His uncle looked at me. "You still can't have it!" he said.

"Can't have what?" Casey asked.

Now I knew that voice! It was him! Uncle Marvin was the old guy with the wool hat. He was the man who had caught Teddy Larrabee's lucky birthday baseball!

"It's no use trying to chummy up with my nephew," said Uncle Marvin. "The ball still isn't for sale."

Casey looked at me, then at his great-uncle, then at me again. "What's going on?"

"This is the little whippersnapper who came begging for my home run ball," said Uncle Marvin.

"I didn't beg," I said. "The player who hit the ball wanted it back. That's all."

"Sixty years I've been going to ball games. I never caught a home run ball once in all those years. The second I do, some kid tries to con it off me. Now he's sniffin' around my house for it."

"It's just a coinkydink . . . uh, a coincidence!" I said. "I'm not sniffing. Casey invited me over to see his baseball cards."

"So it's my nephew's cards you're after!" He leaped up and pointed his pen at me. "You'd better stay away from those cards, if you know what's good for you!"

"No!" said Casey. "I *invited* Chad over, Uncle Marvin. I told him he could see the cards. He didn't even ask."

"I didn't know you were his great-uncle. Promise," I said. "I don't want your baseball, either."

"Hmm . . . All right, then." The old man sat down. "It was just a surprise, seeing you barge into the kitchen like that."

"I can see why you want to keep the ball," I

told him. "Sixty years is a long time. How many games have you seen?"

"Too many to count," he said. "I've been to at least fifty ballparks, major and minor. If they have seats in home run territory, that's where I sit. I've always wanted to catch a home run ball. Ever since I was a kid in Chicago. Me and Carl—that's my brother, Casey's grandfather—me and Carl would stand out on Waveland Avenue trying to catch balls hit out of Wrigley Field. I never got one. But Carl did." He had a faraway look in his eyes. "I wonder if he still has that ball."

"He sure does," said Casey. "Granddad shows it to me every single time we see him, and he tells me the story every time. It was hit by—"

"Andy Pafko, I know," said Uncle Marvin. "I remember. Carl wanted him to sign that ball more than anything, but about a week later Pafko was traded to Brooklyn. Broke Carl's heart. Pafko was his favorite player." The old man sighed loudly.

"Are you OK?" Casey asked him.

"Just a lot of memories," said Uncle Marvin.

We went upstairs to see Casey's cards. He had just about everything I had, but a lot more of the older ones. It was incredible.

"Name a team, a year, and a position," he told me.

"Cardinals, 1982, second base."

He went to a box and came up with a card for a player named Tom Herr.

We played that game about fifty more times before it started to get old.

Casey did have more cards than me, but I'll bet he didn't have any *magic* cards. I kept my favorite cards in a red binder. Some of the Pines thought the cards in there helped them work miracles on the field. I gave Mike Stammer my Rafael Furcal card and he turned a triple play all by himself. Lance Pantaño finished a perfect game with a little help from my Jim Bunning card. Sammy Solaris even stole a base after I gave him my Bengie Molina card. That might not seem like a big deal unless you've seen Sammy run. The pine trees outside Pine City Park could beat him in a footrace. I didn't think the cards were really magic, but they reminded players what was possible. Too bad there wasn't a card that would help Teddy Larrabee get his lucky baseball back.

"Do you think your uncle would trade that baseball for anything?" I asked Casey.

"No way," he replied. "Not even for Granddad's ball from Waveland Avenue."

"Hey, how come your uncle Marvin didn't

know he still had that ball?" I asked him. "If your granddad talks about it all the time, wouldn't your uncle Marvin know?"

"They don't talk much," he said. "Dad says they had a falling-out years ago."

"Over what?"

"I don't know. Before we moved to Pine City, we barely knew Uncle Marvin."

"That's too bad." I had always wanted a brother. I figured we'd be best friends.

Casey put his cards away. "I'm missing a few cards," he admitted. "For example, that guy who hit Granddad's home run ball? Andy Pafko? I don't have any cards for him. I sure wish I did. They're hard to find and worth a lot."

"That was a long time ago."

"A really long time ago," he agreed.

• • •

I checked my own cards when I got home. I didn't think I had Andy Pafko. I did have some cards from the 1950s that Grandpa had collected as a kid, but not every player for every team, every year, the way Casey did.

I had my grandpa's cards in a box, not a binder. I flipped through it, looking for Cubs. I nearly missed Andy Pafko because on the card he was a Brooklyn Dodger. The front of the card called him Andy Pafko, and the back called him Andrew. I also noticed a big number one inside the baseball graphic on the back. That made it the first card in the series for that year.

It was a cool card. I definitely didn't want to trade it. I never traded my cards, anyway. I especially never traded the ones that used to belong to Grandpa or Uncle Rick. Sometimes I gave them away and sometimes I lent them to people, but that was different. I didn't want to

trade this one. It was fun to think about what I *could* trade it for, though. I could make Casey wear a Porcupines' cap for a year. I could make him go to a game against the Rogues and cheer for the Pines. Maybe I could get him to wear a Pines' cap for a day just to let him see the card.

I cackled like an evil supervillain in a movie.

6

The Porcupines came home for the last weekend of the regular season. According to Dad, Friday counted as a school night, so I couldn't work. I made up for it by getting to the ballpark early on Saturday. I even made coffee. The coffee machine used to scare me, but I got over that.

Teddy Larrabee was the first player to show up. He helped himself to a cup of coffee.

"Did you have a good birthday?" I asked him.

"The guys took me out for pizza," he said.

"But I'm still pretty bummed about losing that ball."

"Yeah, that's a drag." I could have told him that I had found the guy who caught it, but what was the point? Uncle Marvin would never sell the ball.

"Maybe you miscounted?" I suggested. "Maybe you counted one hit twice or forgot one? You can't be sure that ball was exactly number eight hundred twenty-three, not if you started counting when you were in T-ball."

"Yes, I can," Teddy said. "Because I wrote 'em all down." He pointed at his notebook. "I've been keeping track."

"Really? Even when you were a kid?"

"Yep."

He handed me the notebook. It was the spiral-bound kind, with the narrow line spacing that teachers seemed to like. On the first page

the printing was big and loopy like a little kid's writing.

May 7. Today I got a hit!

May 13. I got another hit!

I flipped through the notebook pages. The handwriting gradually got smaller and neater as Teddy grew up. Every page was full of base hits. About halfway through he had started adding other info: the inning, the opposing team, the pitcher's name, what the game situation was, and what happened next.

July 17. 2B off Cole Robinson of Somerset. 3rd inning, one out, nobody on. Left on base.

Even with more than 800 hits, Teddy hadn't gotten through the first section of the notebook. I flipped to the last entry in the book. It was hit number 823.

"You haven't gotten a hit since your birthday?" That was like six or seven straight games without a hit.

"Nope," Teddy answered. "Ever since I lost that lucky baseball, I've been in the worst slump. I was hoping that you could look for that fan who caught it? He might be sitting in the same section today. Maybe I can cut a deal."

"Actually, I already did find him," I said, and I told him about Uncle Marvin. "He's been waiting sixty years for that ball. He won't trade it for anything."

"I respect that," said Teddy. "I just hope I can break out of this slump without the ball."

"Of course you can," I told him.

"I sure hope so," he said. "I have a lot of blank pages in that notebook. I plan on filling them all before I'm done."

• • •

Teddy was zero for four that day. Grumps, the Pines' manager, took him out for a pinch hitter in the seventh inning. The next day, Grumps put Luis Quezada at first base. Luis was a utility infielder and pinch runner. The only bright side for Teddy was that Luis didn't get a hit, either. Teddy was back at first in the next game, but he still didn't get any hits.

• • •

"Remember that Andy Pafko card?" I told Casey after school on Tuesday. We were walking to his house.

"You mean the card you made up?"

"I did not."

"Did so."

"I've got it right here," I told him. I patted my backpack. The card was tucked inside my math book.

"Prove it," Casey said. "Seeing is believing. But before you ask, I already told you: I'm not wearing a Porcupines' cap, even for five seconds."

"I know," I said. "I just want to see Uncle

Marvin's home run ball." I thought maybe once we had the ball and the card out, I could talk Uncle Marvin into trading the ball for the card. I hated to do it, but Teddy needed the ball more than I needed the card.

"That's fair," Casey said.

We went in through the kitchen. Uncle Marvin was doing another crossword and listening to a game on the radio.

"Uncle Marvin, can Chad see your home run ball?"

He looked up from his crossword. "Hmm. All right. I guess I trust you now."

"Awesome." I started following him out of the kitchen.

"You wait right here," he said. "I still don't want you to know where it's hidden. A guy can't be too careful."

I unzipped my backpack and took out my

math book. The radio was blaring a big league game from Chicago.

We heard something heavy being moved in the other room, and then we heard Uncle Marvin shout, "*Gabbagah!*"

A moment later he appeared, wagging his finger at me. "You already took it!" he cried.

"What? How could I? I've only been here twice. Casey was with me every second."

"All I know is that my home run ball is missing!" Uncle Marvin sat down and took some deep breaths.

"Maybe you just forgot where you put it," said Casey. "It *was* more than a couple of weeks ago."

"Nonsense. I know exactly where I put it. It was in a shoebox on top of the china hutch."

"Let me look for it, Uncle Marvin," said Casey.

"Fine."

"Can I help?" I offered.

"Can he?" Casey asked his uncle.

"I suppose," he said. "I guess he didn't take it. But somebody did."

We started in the dining room. I found the shoebox on top of the china hutch, but sure enough, it was empty. We searched the living room and also Uncle Marvin's study.

Uncle Marvin searched his own bedroom. When we went to the porch, Arthur started screeching and showing us his claws.

"Arthur likes the porch," said Casey. "It's his territory. That's why I never use the front door."

"At least we know nobody else got in that way," I said.

Fortunately, there weren't many places on the porch to look—just a beat-up armchair that had been slashed to ribbons and a scratching post in perfect condition.

We couldn't find the baseball anywhere. When I left, Uncle Marvin had his head in his hands and was groaning. I decided it wasn't a good time to show him the Andy Pafko card.

Wayne Zane was right about one thing. Teddy's lucky baseball didn't seem to bring good luck to anybody.

he Porcupines finished the season in fourth place. Because of the seeding, they would play the Rogues in the first round of the playoffs. The series would open in Rosedale. Then the games would move to Pine City Park for the weekend.

I wasn't as happy as I thought I'd be. Sure, I could work at least one playoff game, but what if the Porcupines lost the series? Even worse, what if they lost at home? The thought of the Rosedale Rogues winning the series in Pine City Park almost made me sick to my stomach.

"Sorry. I know that you guys like the Porcupines," Casey told me and Dylan at lunch. "But the Rogues are just a better team in every category."

"No, they aren't," I said.

"Hitting, pitching, fielding—no matter how you slice it, the Rogues are better," Casey replied.

I knew he'd win any of those arguments, what with his DIPS and OPS. But I knew something he didn't. "The Porcupines have better personalities."

"What?"

"Sorry, it's true," I told him. "The Rogues are stuck-up."

"Says you!"

"I worked with them," I reminded him. "They made fun of the ballpark, the team, and the town. Tell him, Dylan."

Dylan looked up from his book—he was still reading about cells. "The Rogues can come across as stuck-up," he agreed.

"Well, maybe it's hard not to be stuck-up when you're the best," said Casey. "Anyway, they aren't all stuck-up. Damien Ricken isn't stuck-up."

"He's the worst one of all!" I said.

"Why? What did he say?"

"He said Pine City was all pines and no city."

Casey laughed. "Well, Damien's from New York. He's used to a big city."

"He also complained that you can't get catfish and hush puppies at the ballpark."

"That's all? Have the catfish and hush puppies they sell at the Rosedale ballpark sometime. Then you'll know why he said that."

"Fine!" I told Casey. "Everything is better in

Rosedale. But the Rogues didn't have to trash Pine City while I was sitting right there."

"Yeah," said Dylan. "They did that to me too. They said the Porcupine logo looked like a hedgehog. They also said Victor Snapp wasn't fit to hold the microphone for their announcer."

"They made fun of Victor Snapp?" I couldn't believe it. Their stuck-up-ed-ness had no limits. Victor Snapp was the best announcer in the league!

"The Rogues made fun of pretty much everything at Pine City Park," said Dylan. "Except for Spike."

"Nobody would make fun of Spike," I said.

Spike was the junior mascot, a funny-looking porcupine kid everybody loved. Not many people knew what Dylan and I knew about Spike. We knew that our classmate Abby was inside the Spike costume.

"Damien Ricken did say that Myung Young was the best defensive player in the Prairie League," Dylan continued. "Plus Ricken said he'd give anything to have Ryan Kimball saving his games. Oh, and he said he liked you."

"Me?" I asked.

"Yeah," Dylan replied. "Ricken told me, 'I want the kid who was here yesterday. I liked him.' Nice way to make *me* feel welcome. Ricken said the pizza place you recommended was great. He said it was the best pizza he'd had since he left Long Island." Dylan went back to reading his book.

"So maybe he's not *completely* stuck-up," I admitted.

Abby came over to our table and sat across from me and Casey.

"Hi, Chad! Hi, Dylan!"

"Hey," I said. "Are you excited about the game on Saturday?"

"Eeep. I can't go. I have play practice."

"Huh? You're not going to be there? We *need* Spike!" Abby was a great junior mascot.

"I'm really sorry!" she said. "I can't do both."

"How are the Porcupines going to win without you?" I asked. I felt like the junior mascot was part of the magic that had turned the Porcupines into a playoff team.

"I'm really sorry," said Abby.

"Huh?" Casey looked confused. "Why would the Porcupines lose without you?"

"She's their best player," said Dylan.

"Kind of a secret weapon," I agreed.

"Guys!" Abby said.

"It's OK. He can keep a secret," I said. I leaned in and whispered, "Abby is the designated pitcher."

"There's no such thing," said Casey.

"That's what makes her such a great secret weapon."

• • •

Since the first game was in Rosedale, I went
to Casey's house to listen to it on the radio.
I brought my homework with me. It was the
only way Mom and Dad would let me go.

Dylan was already in the living room,
munching on popcorn.

"You're here too?" I said in surprise. Dylan
was a batboy, but he wasn't a big baseball fan.

"Well, I might have to break up a fight
between you and Casey," he joked.

A black blur leaped from the sill between
the living room and the porch and landed on
the back of the couch. It was Arthur, the scary
black cat that almost never left the porch. He
took a couple of swipes at the cushion, which
was already in shreds, then hopped onto Dylan's
lap.

Dylan gave the cat's head a scratch, and
Arthur started to purr.

Casey stared. "That cat hates everybody!"

"This guy? Come on," said Dylan.

Arthur raised his chin so Dylan could stroke his neck.

"He sure doesn't like me," said Uncle Marvin. "And I feed him every day."

"He doesn't like me, either," said Casey.

"That cat scares me," I said.

Dylan rubbed the cat's ears. "Who's the big bad cat?" he asked.

Arthur just purred louder.

asey's parents were out looking at houses. Uncle Marvin made us sloppy joes, which were pretty good. Dylan had a hard time eating his with Arthur on his lap. Arthur was purring so loudly that Casey had to turn up the radio. The game was tied, 0–0, after four innings. Both Lance Pantaño and Damien Ricken were pitching a great game.

After dinner, Casey and I did our homework at the coffee table. Dylan had to prop up a textbook on his knee so he could do his math problems. Arthur was still in his lap, eyes closed and purring up a storm. The game remained scoreless after eight innings. It was nearly time to go home, so I hoped the Porcupines scored soon.

"I bet the Rogues get a walk-off win in the bottom of the ninth," said Casey. "I'd love to see it. I would be there in person if we hadn't moved!"

"Don't worry. They won't," I said. I hoped I was right.

Arthur finally woke up. He stood up in Dylan's lap, stretched, then jumped to the floor and wandered off.

"Nice cat," said Dylan. "But I think my leg fell asleep." He jiggled it.

Casey's mom and dad came in. They went on and on about a house they had seen. "There's a great room for you," Casey's mom told him. "It's got built-in shelves for all your baseball cards."

"Hold on. Something just happened." Casey turned up the radio. You could hear crowd noise. None of us had been paying attention.

The announcer was talking over a hiss of noise: "The scoreless game is finally broken up by—"

"Hurrah!" Casey pumped his fist.

"Sammy Solaris!" the commentator said. "And the Porcupines take a one-run lead in the top of the ninth."

"Drat!" Casey put his arms down. "I thought the Rogues were still batting."

I was biting my nails when Ryan Kimball came out to pitch the bottom of the ninth. It was still 1–0.

"Kimball's really good," I told Casey. "Even

your man Damien Ricken said so. What about that?"

"I know. But the game's not over till it's over," he said.

Ryan Kimball got three straight outs, and the Porcupines won, 1–0.

Casey chewed on his lower lip for a second. "I was sure the Rogues would win with Ricken pitching," he said.

I tried not to smirk. "Ricken did pitch really well. Lance just pitched better. Ryan too."

"Whatever. Tomorrow we'll win by ten runs," he predicted.

The next night, Dylan and Casey came to listen at my house. Mom made fish sticks and fries. Penny spent the whole evening letting Dylan pet her. The Rogues won, 3–2.

"I thought they'd win by more," said Casey.

I was disappointed the Porcupines had lost,

but I was feeling better about the playoffs. "I told you. The Porcupines are better than you think."

• • •

I'd been to games that were sold out, but Pine City Park felt twice as full and five times as loud on Saturday. It was a lot of fun to run out on the field during batting practice. Dylan and I got a huge round of applause, as if we were players.

"Do you want to work with the Pines for both playoff games?" Dylan asked me. "You've been living for this."

"Nah, it wouldn't be fair. Besides, I want the Rogues to sign a baseball."

"You're getting a signed ball for Casey?"

"Sure. It might make him feel better after the Porcupines win the series."

"Yeah," Dylan said with a laugh. "It'll be

fun, whatever happens." He high-fived me and went to the Pines' dugout. I circled around the diamond to the visitors' dugout.

The regular Porcupines mascot, Pokey, was walking around with a gigantic tube stuffed with T-shirts. He fired them into the stands. The fans scrambled for them, but they didn't seem as excited as usual.

Then a slow chant started up. "Spike! Spike! Spike!" The fans wanted to see the junior mascot. I knew it was a waste of time. Abby was at school, practicing her school play.

"Spike couldn't be at today's game because of important porcupine business elsewhere," said Victor Snapp, the announcer. But it didn't seem to make much difference.

"Spike! Spike! Spike!"

The crowd was still chanting when I got to the opposing team's dugout. The Rogues were quiet and nervous. They weren't even complaining about the ballpark.

I passed the ball around for signatures, and made sure the Rogues all knew it wasn't for me.

"Sure you're not switching sides?" Damien Ricken asked me.

"No way! I'm a Porcupines' fan through and through." I remembered how I rooted against the Pines for two weeks and felt a twinge of guilt.

"Any fan of baseball and good pizza is all right by me," said Damien. He signed the ball. Maybe he wasn't such a bad guy.

"So, what can you tell me about this lefty?" the Rogues' catcher asked me.

"Not much." The starting pitcher for the Porcupines was named Kyle Kostelnik. I hadn't talked to Kyle even once since he joined the team. "He's good, though."

"I hate hitting against lefties," the catcher grumbled. He did not look happy.

Kyle got the first three Rogue batters out in the top of the first. I started to feel hopeful. I got even more hopeful in the bottom half of the inning. The Porcupines scored two runs, loaded the bases, and still didn't have any outs. Teddy Larrabee came up to bat. I crossed all of my fingers and toes. A base hit would blow the game wide open.

But Teddy grounded into a double play. The third run scored, but you could feel all the energy get sucked right out of the ballpark.

The Porcupines didn't score again the whole game, and the Rogues wound up winning, 5–3. The catcher hit a three-run homer in the fifth inning. He must not have hated hitting against lefties *that* much.

The Rogues were a lot less nervous after

the game. They were now one win away from clinching the series, after all. Plus their pitching coach had cleared Damien Ricken to start the next day. Usually pitchers take four days between starts. Damien only had three, but a lot of stuff changed in the playoffs.

"We'll wrap this thing up tomorrow," said one of the Rogues.

ost of the Porcupines were gone by the time I got to the locker room. Those who were still there talked about big hits they didn't get and the line drives they didn't catch.

"It's my fault," said Teddy. "I snuffed that rally in the first inning. I'm zero for whatever, the whole series. I haven't had a hit in weeks. If Grumps had anyone else, I would be out of the lineup."

"It's not all on you," said Wayne Zane.

"It's mostly on me," said Teddy. "I know it."

"The series isn't over," Tommy said. "Sheesh. If we win tomorrow, the series will be tied."

"Yeah . . . with game five back at Rosedale," said Sammy. "Plus Ricken is pitching tomorrow."

"Then so am I."

We all looked over at Lance Pantaño. I hadn't even realized he was still there.

"Are you ready to pitch on three days' rest?" Wayne asked him.

"I will be," Lance replied. "Now, where's my coffee mug?"

● ● ●

"Want to go with me to Casey's?" I asked Dylan when we were done. "I want to give him his ball."

"He didn't come to the game?"

"Nah. He said his parents were so busy house-hunting, they didn't get tickets in time.

He's coming tomorrow with the whole family. He said he was sure the Rogues would win today and he wanted to see them take the series." I figured Casey would be twice as smug tomorrow if the Rogues did win, so I wanted to get this over with.

"Sure, I'll go," said Dylan. "It's not that late. It'll be nice to see Arthur."

Arthur was even happier to see Dylan. The cat meowed and rubbed his head against Dylan's legs.

"That's a good kitty." Dylan crouched to stroke the cat's head. Arthur purred happily.

"With you, he is," said Uncle Marvin.

Arthur suddenly leaped onto the couch, through the window, and out to the porch. He loped back into the room with something in his mouth. He dropped it at Dylan's feet.

"A present? For me?" Dylan picked up a wet, chewed-up, clawed-up, slobbery lump.

"My home run ball!" said Uncle Marvin. "I told you somebody stole it."

"Thank you," Dylan told the cat. He handed the ball to Uncle Marvin and then knelt to give Arthur a good belly rub.

"Well, it's been chewed up and spat out," said Uncle Marvin, looking at the ball. "But I'm glad to have it back." He got a kitchen towel and wiped off the ball. He hummed while he worked.

"Would you sell it now?" I asked him. "I know Teddy really wants it back."

"No, sir!" the old man said.

"But it's important." I explained about Teddy's slump. "He thinks he needs the baseball back or he'll never get another hit."

"That's silly," said Casey.

"It's true *because* he thinks it," I told him. "That's how baseball players are."

"I don't know," said Uncle Marvin. "I can see why your friend needs it, but this ball means a lot to me."

"He said he'd give you a hundred bucks," I said.

"Ah, what would I do with a hundred dollars?" asked Uncle Marvin. "I've already got a hundred dollars."

"What about a trade? I have a card of that guy who used to play for the Cubs. The one who hit the homer your brother caught."

Uncle Marvin shot up straight in his chair. "You have an Andy Pafko baseball card?"

"Yeah, him. He's a Dodger on the card, though. Is that OK?"

"Holy Zamboni!" said Uncle Marvin. He jumped up and peered out the window, then closed the blinds. He came back and whispered, "You can't be too careful. Kid, I want to level with you. I want that card, and I want it bad. It may be the one thing on earth I want more than this home run ball. Can I see it?"

"I don't have it here," I said.

"We'll go to your house, then," said Uncle Marvin. "I'll drive."

I groaned. "I don't have it at home, either. It's in my desk at school." It was my teacher's fault. She didn't give us any math homework that weekend, and the Andy Pafko card was still at school, tucked between the pages of my math book. I had gotten used to looking at the card as I was making my way through math problems. "You can do it!" Andy's face always seemed to say.

"Hmm. That does complicate things," said Uncle Marvin.

"If you give me the ball now, I'll bring you the card on Monday," I promised. "Teddy could really use it for the game tomorrow."

"Don't do it!" said Casey. "Don't help the Porcupines, Uncle Marvin!"

"I'd rather have the card by tomorrow, anyway," said Uncle Marvin.

I glanced at the clock. There might be time. If the rehearsal was still going on, Ms. Henry would be there, and I could ask her to let me into the classroom.

"We need to go to the school," I said.

"I'll drive you," said Uncle Marvin.

"I'm coming too," said Casey.

"To the batboymobile!" said Dylan.

10

The barboymobile turned out to be a huge Buick from caveman times. All three of us fit in the back with room to spare. Unfortunately, to Uncle Marvin, "hurrying" meant going five miles below the speed limit. I just hoped we didn't show up to find the doors locked and the school empty.

We were in luck. One of the gym doors was open. I went inside and saw Abby on the stage, reading from a script. "I'm so cold," she said with a shiver. "My hands are numb." The way she said it made *me* feel cold.

"Very nice," said Ms. Henry.

I hustled across the gym to the stage.

"Chad?" said Ms. Henry. "The play is already cast, but if you really want to be in it, I *could* use more boys—"

"How did the game go?" Abby interrupted. "Did the Porcupines win?"

"I'll think about it," I told Ms. Henry. I turned to Abby. "We lost and the crowd was chanting for Spike."

I turned back to Ms. Henry. "Can you please let me into the classroom for ten seconds? I have a math emergency."

Ten minutes later, I was back in the batboymobile with my math book.

"I'm in the play," I told Dylan and Casey. "I felt like I owed Ms. Henry, so I agreed to be in it. She needed boys."

"What role?" Dylan asked.

"Passerby number three." At least I was a human being this time.

"Let's see the card," said Uncle Marvin. I flipped through the pages of my math book until I found the Andy Pafko card. I gave it one last look. I liked this card . . . and it had been one of Grandpa's.

I thought about Teddy's notebook, and all those blank pages waiting to be filled with hits.

I looked at Uncle Marvin. He was trembling with excitement.

I looked at the card. "You can do it, kid!" Andy Pafko seemed to say.

I reached out and gave the card to Uncle Marvin.

"It's just like I remember it," he said. He flipped it over. "It's got a red back too. Just like Carl's. I'd forgotten about that. Pafko was a

Dodger by the time he got a card. Carl liked it anyhow." The old man gulped.

Casey leaned forward from the back. "Carl? You mean Granddad?"

"That's who I mean," said Marvin. "When I was ten years old, I got my first bike. It was a Schwinn Panther. That was a beautiful bike, boys. They don't make them like that anymore. Mine was royal blue, and I liked it because it was the same color as the Cubs' uniforms. I took that bike out and I was on top of the world for all of five minutes. Then I saw another boy on the exact same bike. He had playing cards fastened to the spokes of the front wheel with clothespins, and it made his bike sound like a motorbike. Well, suddenly my bike didn't seem so hot. I wanted to do the same thing to my spokes. What I did was a horrible thing."

Uh-oh. I knew where this story was going. But I didn't say anything. Uncle Marvin kept talking.

"I didn't dare take Dad's playing cards, but my brother, Carl, had a cigar box full of baseball cards. I grabbed a handful. Carl wasn't home, and I figured I'd put them back before he knew they were gone. I shouldn't have done it, but that's what I did. I didn't even look to see who was on the cards."

"Was Andy Pafko one of them?" I asked.

"He was. I rode all over the neighborhood, across muddy lawns, and through puddles. The cards were all wrecked. I realized I was in big trouble, so I threw them all away. When Carl asked about them, I said I didn't know anything. He knew I was lying, and I never fessed up."

"And that's why you two don't talk now?" Casey guessed.

"That's not the only reason, but I feel like that's where it all started," Marvin said. "Well, Carl is coming for the game tomorrow. I can make a lot of amends if I give him this card. 'Handy Andy' was his favorite player. Carl could put it on display with his ball . . ." Uncle Marvin sniffed. "Yeah, that's worth more to me than my home run ball. I guess you've got a deal."

"Good," I said, but I didn't feel good. I was doing the right thing—helping Teddy and helping Uncle Marvin—but I was going to miss that card. Especially when I did math problems.

11

eddy was confused when I handed
him the wreck of his home run ball.
"What's this?" he asked.

"Your lucky birthday baseball," I told him.
"The guy who caught it has a cat."

"You must mean a cougar," said Teddy.

"For a lucky baseball, that thing sure doesn't
look like it's had much luck," said Wayne Zane.
"Just sayin'."

"It's the right ball, though," said Teddy. "I
can feel it." He tossed it in the air and caught
it. "I feel luckier already. This ball has been

through a lot, but it's still here. Just like us Porcupines."

"Let me hold it for a second," said Tommy. "I could use some good luck." He took it, gripped it, smiled, and then handed it to Sammy.

The Pines passed the ball around. Everybody squeezed a bit more luck out of it until it got to Lance. He held the beat-up ball, muttered something softly in Spanish, and then gave it back to Teddy.

"We're going to win today," Lance said. "I just know it."

• • •

Spike was back! The junior mascot and Pokey did some of their best bits from the season: Spike and the radio; Spike and the water balloons; Spike learning how to drive the golf cart. The crowd loved it.

That gave me time to go see Casey and his family. His granddad and Uncle Marvin were sitting next to each other. They were practically twins. Carl even had a matching wool cap.

"Is this the kid you swindled out of that card?" Casey's granddad said.

"I told you, I didn't know," said Uncle Marvin.

"Didn't know what?" I asked. Did Uncle Marvin give me the wrong baseball? If so, I wasn't telling Teddy and the team. Not after they had passed the ball around for good luck.

"Tell him, Marvin," said Carl.

"I didn't know," he grumbled. "I never would have taken it if I'd known."

"What's going on?" I asked.

Casey jumped up to explain. "Granddad says the Andy Pafko card is worth a small fortune. It's one of the most valuable baseball cards there is. So he's making Uncle Marvin give it back to you."

"Really?" I didn't care how much the card was worth, but I was getting it back? I couldn't believe my luck. "Does that mean Uncle Marvin wants the home run ball back?"

Casey shrugged.

I looked at Uncle Marvin, who shrugged, too. "Keep it. I think Arthur misses it more than I do."

"I'll get you another ball, at least," I offered.

"Bah. It's not the same if I don't catch it," said Uncle Marvin. "But I go to a lot of games, and I'm young yet."

"It was nice of him to trade for the card for me," said Carl. "That was a nice gesture."

"It was the least I could do," said Uncle Marvin.

• • •

Lance got everybody out in the first two innings, but Damien was just as good. In the bottom of the second he had two outs, and two strikes on Teddy Larrabee. It looked like the game would go just like the first game in the series.

Then the Bear got a bloop hit. That means a lucky hit. The ball just kind of landed between the Rogues' shortstop and the second baseman. Either one of them could have picked it up and thrown to first, but neither of them did. They both thought the other would do it. They looked at each other for a second—and that was long enough for Teddy to scamper to first base.

It was just a two-out single, and a lucky one, but it felt like a big deal. The Porcupines had gotten to Damien Ricken!

The Rogues' pitcher shook his head, got a new ball, and struck out Danny O'Brien. Teddy didn't even score, but his one hit—his first hit in two weeks—got the fans clapping and chanting.

The Rogues got a leadoff walk in the third inning. The base runner then stole second. It was just one potential run out there, but today one run felt like a hundred.

Lance was calm. He walked the next batter, too. There was still nobody out. Down at the end of the bench, Grumps the manager watched with no expression on his face.

"Double play," Sammy whispered. "Come on, double play." A second later the batter hit a bouncing ball toward the shortstop. Mike Stammer fielded it and tossed it to George "President" Lincoln at second base for one out. The President threw it to Teddy at first base for the second out. "Yeah!" Sammy pumped his fist. "I told ya!"

Grumps still looked blank. He could have been waiting for a bus.

Now there was a Rogues' runner on third and two outs. I felt a lot better, but the go-ahead run was too close for comfort.

"You're grinding your teeth," Sammy told me. "Calm down."

"Sorry." I hadn't even realized I was doing it.

"Never mind. That was me," said Sammy.

The batter hit a hot smash toward Mike. He dived, snagged the ball, got up, and fired it to first. The umpire called the runner out, and the Rogues' manager rushed over to argue. The argument went on for a few minutes, and the crowd started to get restless. Pokey and Spike ran out to mimic the argument. Pokey looked stern while Spike pretended to complain, kicked dirt, and gestured wildly. Pokey finally threw his thumb back over his shoulder—the sign that someone was thrown out of the game. The crowed cheered, playing along, while Spike stormed off.

Meanwhile, the Rogues' manager really *was* thrown out of the game. He glowered and started to stalk off the field, but Spike ran after him. The manager realized something was going on, stopped, and turned around. Spike gave him a big, consoling, porcupine hug. The crowd cheered wildly. It was the funniest thing Spike had ever done. The manager did calm down and even patted Spike's spiny head. I had tears in my eyes, I was laughing so hard. Even Grumps was smiling. I decided that even if the Porcupines lost, this was the greatest game ever.

12

In the bottom of the ninth inning, Myung and Mike hit singles and Sammy walked. That put a Porcupine on first, second, and third base. Teddy came up to bat with the bases loaded and two outs. The Rogues changed pitchers after the walk. Damien Ricken went back to the dugout looking miserable.

"Good game, though," I said out loud. I clapped along with the rest of the Porcupines' fans as the new Rogues' pitcher walked to the mound. I didn't know his name, but based on his warm-up pitches he was a knuckleballer. A knuckleball drops and darts and seems to hang in the air like a butterfly. It was a big change from Damien's slider. I hoped the Bear could swat one of those butterflies.

"This is a big one," said Wayne, as if I didn't know. A base hit, and the Porcupines would win the game and tie up the series. Just yesterday, that seemed impossible.

Teddy flailed at the first pitch, missing it by a mile. Then he watched the second one float over the plate for a called strike. The third pitch was a ball.

The Rogues' pitcher wound up and threw the fourth pitch. Teddy kept his eye on the ball, and at just the right moment he swung hard.

The ball sliced down the first base line, a close, very close call . . . *fair ball!* It kept on rolling—all the way to the wall. While the

Rogues' right fielder scrambled to get it, Myung, Mike, and Sammy were racing around the bases.

Myung crossed home plate. Score! The Porcupines had won!

"That's our Bear!" shouted Victor Snapp over the PA system. The crowd roared as the Pines emptied out of the dugout to congratulate their hero. The Porcupines had won, 1–0, thanks to Teddy "the Bear" Larrabee!

• • •

The first thing Teddy did when he got back to the locker room was get out his notebook and start writing in it.

"What's that for?" Wayne asked.

"Why do you need to know?" Teddy asked.

"Just curious," said Wayne.

"I write down all my hits. That's all."

"Oh. OK. Nothing wrong with that."

"It's for my life story," Teddy blurted out. "I figured I should keep count. I also keep a diary, but that's at home. But I write down my hits right after the game so I won't forget."

"Your autobiography?" Tommy looked impressed.

"I have a title for it and everything—*Running with the Bear*. Go ahead and make your jokes. Let's get it over with."

Teddy waited, but nobody said anything. Not even Wayne.

"That's a great title," said Sammy.

"Yeah, if I had anything half that good, I'd write an autobiography," said Wayne.

"I can't wait to read it," said Tommy. "When are you going to finish it?"

"It's my life story," said Teddy. "So I won't be done for a really long time."

• • •

"What a great game!" Dylan said when he got back to the Porcupines' locker room. "I thought I was going to chew my own lip off when Teddy was batting with the bases loaded, and then, BAM!" He mimed the swing and the big hit.

"So you're officially a baseball fan?" I asked him.

"Sure," Dylan replied. "I'll never be as big a fan as you, but today's game was fun. I can't wait for tomorrow's."

Dylan went to his locker. "Hey!" He pulled out a new jersey with signatures all over it.

"Just in case this was our last home game," Wally explained. Wally was the Pines' clubhouse manager, and our boss. "We wanted to get you kids something."

"Look!" Dylan showed me the back of his jersey. Instead of BB, it said CRITTERS. "I guess that's my new nickname," he said. "I love it."

"It suits you," I said. I ran to my own locker. I had a new jersey too. It was signed by all the players and also by Wally, Grumps, Pokey, Spike, and Victor Snapp. It looked like they even had Ernie Hecker sign it! I flipped it over to see the nickname the team had given me:

KID MAGIC.

About the Author

Kurtis Scaletta's previous books include *Mudville*, which *Booklist* called "a gift from the baseball gods" and named one of their 2009 Top 10 Sports Books for Youth. Kurtis lives in Minneapolis with his wife and son and some cats. He roots for the Minnesota Twins and the Saint Paul Saints. Find out more about him at www.kurtisscaletta.com.

About the Artist

Eric Wight was an animator for Disney, Warner Bros., and Cartoon Network before creating the critically acclaimed *Frankie Pickle* graphic novel series. He lives in Doylestown, Pennsylvania, and is a diehard fan of the Philadelphia Phillies and the Lehigh Valley Iron Pigs. You can check out all the fun he is having at www.ericwight.com.

Come on into the *topps* ® Reading Clubhouse!

Check out these other championship titles in the Topps League Story series featuring Chad, Dylan, Spike, and the Pine City Porcupines.